The Adventures of Everyday Geniuses

Keep Your Eye on the Prize

MORECASTER SCHOOL
SCIENCE FAIR

Written by
Barbara Esham

Illustrated by
Mike Gordon

Editor
Tina Raye Dayton

It was the year my class was allowed to participate in the Morecaster School Science Fair.

I was so excited! Not only could we choose our very own topic, but we also each had a chance to win the prize for ...

"Most Interesting Science Project."

3

It was going to be a challenge though...
some of the projects were quite sophisticated.

4

I wondered exactly how much help I would need for the project. Sometimes my mom gets so excited about my school projects that she helps too much.

But there was one thing I was certain of – this science project was going to be 100% my work, or maybe 93% my work, but no less!

I even set up my own private work area in the basement of our home..

It didn't take long to realize that the project was too much for my parents to resist; they wanted to "help".
We needed to create some boundaries...

I worked on my project for weeks. Mary, my older sister, didn't understand why I would not allow Mom and Dad to help. "You'll never get to play on the weekends if you don't let them help you, Dylan," she said, looking up from her magazine — the Tonis Brothers Special Edition, including bonus pictures of course.

Mary really loves the Tonis Brothers...

Don't get the wrong idea. I love to play outside, and sometimes I even avoid the occasional assignment until the last minute...

But for some reason, the science fair project
was all that I could think about.

I worked for weeks...

I was dedicated to every little detail.

Some of my classmates completed their projects early
and brought them to school before the due date.

I tried really hard not to let the other projects make me feel discouraged. It was difficult for me not to compare my project with my classmates' projects, but I tried to keep my mind on what I was doing.

14

Lucky for me, Dr. Swarthmore, the science fair director and our school district's science coordinator, valued every student's hard work.

I knew she would notice the time and effort that each student put into his project.

The BIG day finally arrived!
the Morecaster School Annual Science Fair
was one of the biggest events of the school year.

The auditorium was packed with teachers, parents, students, and, yes... reporters from our town's local newspaper and television station.

I was careful to keep my project safe from the stampede...
I made sure to push it back just a little so it wouldn't
get knocked over.

My sister and her friends were very interested in Christopher Sampson's project. Everyone in my sister's class thinks Christopher looks just like Joe Tonis...

I guess he does, a little.

I felt proud explaining my science project to everyone
who stopped by to see it.

It didn't matter to me if it wasn't the most interesting or
exciting project. I was proud of it, and
I didn't need to compare.

The day was filled with interesting ideas and exciting projects!
David Sheldon created the largest volcano in science fair history...

His parents had to hire a moving company
to bring it in through the delivery entrance.

Katie developed a new spelling system to prove how difficult learning to spell and read can be.

Even the reading teachers from Morecaster Elementary were having a difficult time...

The entire auditorium fell silent when Dr. Swarthmore's voice came over the speaker. "Today has been very exciting for the science committee," she said with a smile.

"I see many future scientists and innovators in our auditorium, along with many unique and interesting projects," she added.

"After much thought and consideration, the science fair committee has decided to recognize the student who best reflects the work ethic of one of history's most famous scientists, Thomas Edison," Dr. Swarthmore announced. "Thomas Edison found happiness and reward in his work without focusing on the final outcome," she added.

"I find my greatest pleasure, and so my reward, in the work that precedes what the world calls success."
- Thomas Edison

"It is with great pride that we honor Dylan Cooper with this year's Morecaster Science Fair first place prize," Dr. Swarthmore announced with a smile.

I almost didn't hear Dr. Swarthmore announce my name.
I was listening of course, but one of my jars tipped over,
and I was trying to fix it.

"Congratulations, Dylan, you and Thomas Edison would have had much in common," she whispered as she placed the award in my hands.

Once the Science Fair was over, I carefully packed up my stuff.

I had a feeling I would remember that day.

I would definitely remember the days leading up to it!

I can't wait until next year's science fair.

I'm already thinking of a new project!

But next year, I'm going to see if my grandparents
can help keep my parents busy while I work.

The travel program on television claims,
"It's the perfect month for a Caribbean cruise!"

So... what do the experts have to say?

From Dr. Edward Hallowell,

New York Times national best seller, former Harvard Medical School instructor, and current director of the Hallowell Center for Cognitive and Emotional Health...

Fear is the great disabler. Fear is what keeps children from realizing their potential. It needs to be replaced with a feeling of I-know-I-can-make-progress-if-I-keep-trying-and-boy-do-I-ever-want-to-do-that!

One of the great goals of parents, teachers, and coaches should be to find areas in which a child might experience mastery, then make it possible for the child to feel this potent sensation.

The feeling of mastery transforms a child from a reluctant, fearful learner into a self-motivated player.

The mistake that parents, teachers, and coaches often make is that they demand mastery rather than lead children to it by helping them overcome the fear of failure.

The best parents are great teachers. My definition of a great teacher is a person who can lead another person to mastery.

~Dr. Hallowell

As a former elementary school teacher, I have all too often seen projects turned in by students that were clearly more the evidence of mom or dad's expertise than the work of the student. In Keep Your Eye on the Prize, Barbara Esham deftly deals with what can be a difficult subject for students or teachers to broach. How do you help parents understand when the help they're giving is too much? Dylan, the main character in this book, has experienced the same issue, yet is able to achieve success in the school science fair with minimal help from outside. More importantly, because he feels ownership of his work, and has developed a true interest in the topic, he learns much more than if mom or dad had fixed every error or polished every rough edge. This book is as valuable for parents and teachers as it is for young people, and is a great way to help everyone understand how to give just the right amount of assistance.

Dr. Corinne Hyde, Professor of Clinical Education
University of Southern California

What was Dylan's Science Fair Project?

Project Title

Does Saltwater Affect Plant Growth?

by: Dylan Cooper

Supply List

(3) Jars

(9) Bean seeds

Saltwater (1/8 cup salt added to 2 cups of fresh water)

Fresh water

Ruler

Journal to record results

Cataloging in Publication Data

Esham, Barbara
Keep Your Eye on the Prize/ written by Barbara Esham; illustrated
by Mike Gordon. – 1st ed. – Baltimore, MD: Mainstream Connections 2014

p. : cm.
(Adventures of everyday geniuses)

ISBN : 9781603363907   LCCN : 2014914080
Audience: Ages 5-10
Summary: Dylan, the main character in this book, is able to achieve success in the school science fair
with minimal help from outside. More importantly, because he feels ownership of his work,
and has developed a true interest in the topic, he learns much more than if mom or dad had fixed
every error or polished every rough edge. This book is as valuable for parents and teachers as it is
for young people, and is a great way to help everyone understand how to give just the right amount
of assistance.

1. Children's stories –Juvenile fiction 2. Self-esteem – Juvenile fiction. 3. School – Juvenile fiction
4. Life skills – Fiction 5. Motivation – Juvenile fiction

PZ7.E74583 L37 2014   2014908045

[Fic] – dc22   1314

THE ADVENTURES OF EVERYDAY GENIUSES BOOK SERIES INCLUDED THE FOLLOWING TITLES:

If You're So Smart, How Come You Can't Spell Mississippi?   ISBN: 9781603364485

Stacey Coolidge's Fancy-Smancy Cursive Handwriting   ISBN: 9781603364621

Mrs. Gorski, I Think I Have the Wiggle Fidgets   ISBN: 9781603364690

Last to Finish: A Story about the Smartest Boy in Math Class   ISBN: 9781603364560

Free Association, Where My Mind Goes During Science Class ISBN: 9781603365468

Keep Your Eye on the Prize   ISBN: 9781603363907

BOOK INFORMATION
Keep Your Eye on the Prize
Written by Barbara Esham illustrated by Mike Gordon
Published by Mainstream Connections Publishing
P.O. Box 398, Perry Hall Maryland 21128

Printed in USA

FIRST EDITION
15 14 13 12 11 10 09 08   01 02 03 04 05 06 07 08

ISBN :   9781603363907   LCCN : 2014914080